JOSIE SMITH
at School

JOSIE SMITH

at School

Magdalen Nabb

illustrations by Pirkko Vainio

Margaret K. McElderry Books
New York

Maxwell Macmillan International
New York   London   Singapore   Sydney

This book is for
LIAM JAMES NABB

Certain words in this story have been changed for American readers
with the author's approval.

First United States Edition 1991
All rights reserved. No part of this book may be reproduced or transmitted in
any form or by any means, electronic or mechanical, including photocopying,
recording, or by any information storage and retrieval system, without permission
in writing from the Publisher.

Margaret K. McElderry Books
Macmillan Publishing Company
866 Third Avenue
New York, NY 10022
Macmillan Publishing Company is part of the
Maxwell Communication Group of Companies.

Text copyright © 1990 by Magdalen Nabb
Illustrations copyright © 1990 by Pirkko Vainio
First published 1990 by William Collins Sons & Co. Ltd.
Published by arrangement with HarperCollins Publishers Ltd.
Printed in the United States of America
10 9 8 7 6 5 4 3 2 1

Library of Congress Cataloging-in-Publication Data
Nabb, Magdalen, date
Josie Smith at school / Magdalen Nabb ; illustrations by Pirkko
Vainio. — 1st U.S. ed.
p.   cm.
Summary: Spirited Josie has adventures and misadventures at
school, where she befriends a foreign student and takes part in the
class play.
ISBN 0-689-50533-7
[1. Schools—Fiction.]   I. Vainio, Pirkko, ill.   II. Title.
PZ7.N125Jol   1991
[Fic]—dc20   91-10970

Contents

Josie Smith's New Teacher

On Sunday night Josie Smith was in the bathtub with soapsuds all over her hair.

"Ow!" she said, when her mom rubbed too hard. "Ow!"

"Keep still," said Josie's mom. "I have to rub hard because you get so dirty. You could grow potatoes in your ears."

"And cabbages?" asked Josie Smith.

"And cabbages," said Josie's mom. "Now lie back while I rinse you."

"Swim me up and down and sing," said Josie Smith.

So Josie's mom swam her up and down the bath and rinsed her hair with jugs of water and sang. Josie Smith sang, too. Then

she got dry. When she was in bed in clean, striped pajamas, Josie Smith said, "Tomorrow, can I have a ribbon in my hair for school?"

"You'll only lose it," said Josie's mom.

"But can I?" said Josie Smith.

"All right," said Josie's mom. "Now go to sleep."

"And tomorrow," said Josie Smith, "can I take a present for the new teacher? Eileen's taking one."

"And everything Eileen does, you have to do," said Josie's mom.

"But *can* I?" said Josie Smith. "I like my new teacher."

"You can take her an apple," said Josie's mom. "But how do you know you like her if she's only coming tomorrow?"

"She came on Friday," said Josie Smith, "when Mrs. Ormerod was reading us a story and she wears nail polish and perfume."

"Does she now?" said Josie's mom, and she smiled. "Now go to sleep. Ginger's asleep already. Look."

"I can't see him," said Josie Smith. "Move his basket nearer the bed."

Josie's mom moved Ginger's basket and Ginger opened one eye and said, "Eeeiow," and then went to sleep again.

"Why does Ginger say *eeeiow* instead of meeiow?" asked Josie Smith.

"I don't know," said Josie's mom. "Now go to sleep."

"Mom?" said Josie Smith.

"What now?" said Josie's mom.

"Will the new teacher know I'm the best at reading and writing?"

"She might," said Josie's mom. "I expect Mrs. Ormerod will have told her."

"I'm going to write a story for her," said Josie Smith, "in my best writing with no erasing because I haven't got an eraser."

"You won't be in a fit state to write anything tomorrow," said Josie's mom, "if you don't get to sleep. It's late."

"I am getting to sleep. Mom?"

"That's enough now," said Josie's mom. "I'm going down."

"But *Mom*! Can I have a pencil with an eraser at the end like Eileen's?"

"We'll see."

"But can I?"

"I said we'll see. Now go to sleep. I've got some sewing to finish. Good night."

And she switched off the light.

"Good night!" shouted Josie Smith. Then she whispered to Ginger, "I'm going to think of a story now so I can start it as soon as I get to school."

Josie Smith lay in the dark and thought. She thought of a story with a giant in it. The giant lived in a tower on the top of a hill and when he tried to frighten people he only

4

made them laugh. He was so funny that he made Josie Smith laugh by herself in the dark. She told Ginger about him but Ginger didn't wake up. And downstairs her mom's sewing machine went Tr-r-r-r-r-r-r-ik, tr-r-r-r-r-r-r-ik, tr-r-r-r-r-r-r-ik.

She thought of a better story about a girl who ran away and went to live with the Gypsies. The girl had to sleep in a tent and it was dark and cold and rainy and the girl cried and cried because she wanted her mom. Outside in the night, the rain began pattering at Josie Smith's window and tears came into her eyes when she thought about the girl in the Gypsy's tent. She told Ginger about it but Ginger didn't wake up, and downstairs, her mom's sewing machine went Tr-r-r-r-r-r-r-ik, tr-r-r-r-r-r-r-ik, tr-r-r-r-r-r-ik.

She thought of an even better story with a witch in it. The witch came in at people's windows on rainy nights and stole them when they were asleep. The witch was so frightening that Josie Smith got scared and had to make Ginger wake up to keep her company.

Downstairs, her mom's sewing machine went Tr-r-r-r-r-r-r-ik, tr-r-r-r-r-r-r-ik, tr-r-r-r-r-r-r-ik. Then it stopped. The light came on on the landing and Josie's mom came up to bed.

"Sh-h!" said Josie Smith to Ginger, and she shut her eyes to pretend she was asleep and then she really was asleep.

"Wake up!" said Josie's mom. "Josie! Didn't you hear me shouting?"

"Is it morning?" said Josie Smith.

"Of course it's morning," said Josie's

mom. "You're going to be late for school if you don't hurry up."

Then Josie Smith remembered the new teacher and got dressed as fast as she could. She was so tired that she didn't want her breakfast and when Eileen from next door came to call for her she hadn't got her coat on.

"Hurry up!" said Josie's mom.

Josie Smith got her coat and ran to the front door. Then she came running back.

"My ribbon!" she said. "You promised I could have a hair ribbon!"

"Oh, for goodness' sake," said Josie's mom, and she started looking in the drawers. "Here, this will do."

"I wanted a pink one," said Josie Smith, "like Eileen's."

"You lost the pink one," said Josie's mom, "like you lose them all. This one's better than a pink one because it matches your kilt."

She tied the ribbon tight in Josie Smith's hair and Josie Smith ran to the front door. Then she came running back.

"My apple!" shouted Josie Smith. "You promised I could take an apple for the new teacher!"

"Oh, for goodness' sake," said Josie's mom. "Here. And don't run or you'll drop it on the way."

Josie Smith ran to the front door and opened it. Eileen was waiting for her. She had two pink ribbons in her hair.

Josie Smith and Eileen set off up the street to school.

"I've got a present for the new teacher," Eileen said.

"So have I," said Josie Smith.

"I'll show you if you want," said Eileen, "only you mustn't touch."

They stopped at a corner and Eileen got the present out of her coat pocket. There was a little colored box with tissue paper in it and when Eileen opened the tissue paper very carefully Josie Smith saw a brand new pure white handkerchief with frilly white lace around it and a bunch of pink flowers embroidered in the corner.

"My mom bought it," whispered Eileen, "when she went shopping on

8

Saturday." She folded the tissue paper back
and shut the colored box. Then she said,
"What have you got?"

"An apple," said Josie Smith.

"That's not a real present," Eileen said.

"It is," said Josie Smith. "My mom
said."

"It's not," said Eileen. "Real presents
come from a shop."

"*Well*," said Josie Smith, "apples come
from a shop, anyway."

"You got it from your house," said
Eileen.

"I'm not going to school with you for

being so horrible!" shouted Josie Smith, and she ran off down a back street and hid, holding her apple tight, until Eileen had gone. Then she set off to school by herself.

On the corner next to Josie Smith's school was Mr. Scowcroft's allotment garden, where Josie Smith sometimes went to dig for worms with Gary Grimes. Perhaps Mr. Scowcroft would have something good for a present. Mr. Scowcroft had some flowers growing at the back of his allotment garden. They were called pom-pom dahlias. Josie Smith knew what they were called because Mr. Scowcroft had told her. Mr. Scowcroft was always there in the mornings feeding his hens.

"Mr. Scowcroft!" shouted Josie Smith, holding on to the wire fence. "Mr. Scowcroft! Can I come in?"

But nobody answered. Mr. Scowcroft wasn't there.

Josie Smith thought she'd go in and wait for him. The whistle hadn't gone yet and all the children were playing and shouting in the yard. Mr. Scowcroft's gate was locked but there was a hole in the fence.

Sometimes his hens got out through the hole but they always came back because there was nothing to peck and scratch at in the hard street.

Josie Smith put her apple down and crawled through the hole very carefully so she wouldn't rip her coat. Then she waited for Mr. Scowcroft near the pom-pom dahlias. Most of the pom-pom dahlias were dark red but there were some orange ones and white ones and a beautiful purple one that Josie Smith liked very much. She could ask Mr. Scowcroft for the purple one and then dig up the ground around his lettuces after school. Or else she could dig a bit of it now. All the children were still playing and shouting in the yard but Josie Smith didn't want to play with them. She could dig in the lettuce patch instead while she was waiting.

Josie Smith got the spade that was leaning on the hen shed and started digging. It was hard work because the spade was big and heavy, but the ground was wet and soft and if she stood on the edge of the spade with both her rubber boots it went in.

The children played and shouted in

the yard and Josie Smith dug and dug in the allotment garden until she had dug half the lettuce patch for Mr. Scowcroft. Then she stopped. It was so hot that she had to take her coat off, and it was so quiet that she could hear herself being out of breath. "Phew," she went, "phew-phew-phew." When she got her breath back she said, "That'll be a nice surprise for Mr. Scowcroft."

But Mr. Scowcroft still didn't come.

"I might as well finish all of it," said Josie Smith, "while I'm waiting." So she dug and dug and dug until all the lettuce

patch was done. "Phew," she went, "phew-phew-phew!" Because it was so quiet she could hear herself being out of breath. When she got her breath back she said, "Now it'll really be a surprise for Mr. Scowcroft. I'd better collect the worms for the hens."

Josie Smith didn't like worms. When she came to the allotment garden with Gary Grimes, she did the digging and he collected the worms. She hated doing it by herself but she got the can from near the hen shed and the handkerchief from her pocket and she used the handkerchief to pick up the worms so that she wouldn't feel them wriggling so much. But when she took the can of worms to the hen shed she saw that the hen shed was shut. Josie Smith could hear the hens crowing and scuffling and pecking at the door.

"You want your worms, don't you?" said Josie Smith, putting her face near a crack to talk to them.

The hens crowed and scuffled and pecked at the door.

"I expect you heard me digging and now you're hungry."

The hens crowed and scuffled and pecked even harder at the door. But there was a big piece of wood wedged across the door to keep it shut and it looked very heavy to Josie Smith.

"I'd better wait," Josie Smith told the hens through the crack. "I shouldn't open your shed, anyway, because you're Mr. Scowcroft's hens." The hens went on crowing and scuffling and pecking just the same. Perhaps they were too daft to know whose hens they were. Once, when Josie Smith asked Mr. Scowcroft why the hens pecked at each other, fighting over a worm, and then ran away and forgot to eat it, Mr. Scowcroft said, "Because they're daft."

Josie Smith put the worm can down and went back to look at the purple pom-pom dahlia. She saw a big flower just behind it that wasn't a pom-pom dahlia at all. Josie Smith stood on tiptoe and reached over to pull the big flower's face toward her.

"Ow!" she said. It had prickles. It was a big fat pink rose. When she pulled it toward her it showered rain drops on her face. Josie Smith sniffed. "Perfume!" she

whispered. The rose was soft and cool. But it wasn't Mr. Scowcroft's rose. It had poked its head through the wire fence from behind the allotment garden and come to live with the pom-pom dahlias. Josie Smith had never been behind Mr. Scowcroft's allotment garden. She decided that while she was waiting for Mr. Scowcroft she could go and look where the rose came from.

She crawled out through the hole near the gate where she'd left her apple and went around the corner. There was a vacant lot next to the allotment garden, where they played cowboys and Indians on the way home from school, and a dirt track between the vacant lot and Mr. Scowcroft's fence. Josie Smith went along the dirt track to the end. She saw some steps going down in the long grass and a fence going down beside the steps and a gate at the bottom. Josie Smith stopped and listened but there was nobody coming. It was very quiet. She went down the steps. The gate was locked but there was a gap in the fence near the bottom so Josie Smith squeezed through it and stood looking up at the slope behind Mr. Scowcroft's allotment garden.

There were big white rocks all over the slope and all around the rocks there were blue and white and pink flowers growing. Up at the top were the biggest rose bushes that Josie Smith had ever seen. There were more flowers there even than in Mrs. Crawshaw's flower shop. Josie Smith started to climb up very carefully. Her rubber boots were wet and slippery with mud and she didn't want to slip off the white rocks and squash the blue and white and pink flowers because they were nice. They

were better than buttercups but not as good as bluebells because they didn't smell of anything. Josie Smith went on climbing until she reached the top of the slope right behind the back of the allotment garden. There were hundreds of pale pink roses full of perfume and raindrops.

"Zzzzzzzz," said Josie Smith, and put her face into a big pink rose and drank some drops of bees' drinking water. "Zzzzzzzz."

Josie Smith chose the biggest rose she could see and picked it carefully without pricking her fingers too much. When the twig snapped a shower of water and petals fell on her.

"Zzzzzzzz," said Josie Smith the bee, picking and sniffing and sipping. The soil was very wet under the bushes and her rubber boots sank right in and the petals showered down and covered them. "Pink boots," said Josie Smith, looking down. Then she said, "Zzzzzzzz," and picked some more big pink roses. The thorns scratched her hands and the petals stuck to the scratches like Band-Aids and then she felt something go plop on her head. It was too heavy to be a petal or a drop of bees' drinking water. Josie Smith looked up. The sky was all dirty and dark. Plop! A big squashy raindrop plopped right on Josie Smith's nose. Plop! went another one. Plop plop plop.

"I'd better go now," whispered Josie Smith, "or else I'll get wet. I'll just pick a few more big ones." So she picked a few more big ones and the squashy raindrops went on falling, plopping on the roses and making them nod their heads, bouncing off the leaves and sploshing onto Josie Smith's hands as she chose the best flowers with their petals open wide.

When she couldn't hold any more roses she began to climb down over the rocks in her slippery rubber boots. Once she slipped and hurt her hand but she didn't tread on any of the blue and white and pink flowers.

When she got back to the allotment garden, Mr. Scowcroft still hadn't come. He must have forgotten to come and give the hens their breakfast, Josie Smith thought.

The hungry hens were crowing and scuffling and pecking at the door. I'll

have to give them something to eat,
thought Josie Smith, or else they'll die.
She climbed on an upside-down bucket
and pulled and pulled at the big piece of
wood across the door until it came loose and
fell down. Then she took the can of worms
in to the hens. They crowed and scuffled and
pecked at the worms but there weren't
enough for everybody and some of the hens
didn't get one.

"I could make your breakfast," Josie
Smith said, "because I've seen Mr. Scowcroft
doing it."

But then, all of a sudden, she noticed
how quiet it was. She couldn't hear the
children shouting and playing in the yard
anymore. It had been quiet for a long time.

"I have to go to school," she told the
hens. "I think it might be late now."

But the hens all stood around Josie
Smith, turning their heads to stare at her
with one eye, making soft noises and
pecking at her rubber boots, wanting their
breakfast.

Josie Smith's chest was going bam,
bam, bam. She was frightened of being late

for school, but when she thought of the hens
being shut up by themselves in the dark with
no breakfast a big lump came into her throat
to make her cry. She didn't want the hens to
die. She went out and got the bucket and
started getting the hens' breakfast from the
big bin and mixing it with some water from
the rain barrel. All the time her chest was
going bam, bam, bam. Just when she'd
finished and shut the door and leaned the
piece of wood against it, a voice shouted:

"Josie Smith!"

It wasn't Mr. Scowcroft. It was Mrs.

Scowcroft in a long raincoat and rubber boots and carrying an umbrella.

"Whatever are you doing here at this time?" she said. "It's twenty past nine!"

Twenty past nine! Josie Smith got hold of her roses and ran past Mrs. Scowcroft, through the gate, across the vacant lot, and into the school yard. She crashed in through the front door and went running and skidding in her slippery muddy rubber boots along the corridor, through the cafeteria, and into her classroom. Then she stopped, breathing hard, phew-phew-phew!

Everybody stared. Eileen stared, Gary Grimes stared, and Rawley Baxter stared. All the children at the other tables stared. The new teacher stared. And before anybody could say anything, the door burst open behind Josie Smith and a big voice shouted:

"Where's that child?"

Josie Smith turned around. It was Miss Potts, the principal, and behind her was Mr. Bannister, the caretaker. Miss Potts's face was all red and her eyes were glittery and angry.

"Josie Smith!" she shouted, and Josie Smith's chest went bam, bam, bam. "How *dare* you come running through this school making all that mess in the corridor!"

"And in the hall," said Mr. Bannister, "that's just been polished."

Josie Smith looked at the floor where she'd come in. There was a trail of mud and petals and bits of grass and hen food. Then she looked at her roses. There were no roses left, only the stalks with fuzzy brown lumps on the end of them.

"Excuse me, Miss Valentine," shouted Miss Potts to the new teacher, and she marched in and got hold of Josie Smith's shoulder so hard that it hurt.

"What's your mother thinking of," she roared, "sending you to school at this time and in this state? You're wet through! Where's your coat?"

Josie Smith didn't know.

"Doesn't your mother know any better than to send you out without a coat in this weather? Blow your nose!"

Josie Smith felt in the pocket of her kilt but her handkerchief wasn't there.

"Where's your handkerchief?" roared Miss Potts.

Josie Smith didn't know.

"And what's all that rubbish in your hand?" roared Miss Potts. "Throw it in the wastepaper basket!"

Josie Smith went and threw the stalks in the wastepaper basket.

"All over my floor," said Mr. Bannister.

"Come back here," roared Miss Potts, "and show me your hands!"

Josie Smith showed her muddy hands.

"Go and wash them!" roared Miss Potts, "and your face! And take those

filthy rubber boots off and put your gym shoes on!"

Josie Smith went.

When she came back, Miss Potts was still shouting. She was mad at everybody, now.

"And if any child comes in late again there'll be trouble! Gary Grimes, blow your nose! I've told you all, time and time again, to bring a handkerchief to school! And don't let me hear of any books being torn again in this class or I'll have your parents in! Thank you, Miss Valentine!"

And she marched out. Mr. Bannister went out behind her with his brush.

Josie Smith stood where she was and her chest was going bam, bam, bam, but she was too frightened to cry. She was too frightened to look at the new teacher but she looked at her desk and saw Eileen's present in its box and a bunch of flowers in a vase and three apples. She wondered where her apple was but she couldn't remember. Then the new teacher said quietly, "Go to your place."

Josie Smith went to her table and sat down with Eileen and Gary Grimes and Rawley Baxter. They had to do arithmetic problems. Josie Smith couldn't do the problems. She tried as hard as she could but she couldn't do three minus seven no matter how hard she tried, so when she couldn't try anymore she subtracted the three from the seven and got four. Then she smelled the new teacher's perfume, and a hand with shiny pink nails pointed at the problem in her book.

"You've copied them all down wrongly," the new teacher's voice said.

"You should have added, not subtracted."

At recess it was still raining and they had to stay in. Everybody was noisy and bored and Josie Smith felt tired. Afterward, she had to do all her problems again when the others were all drawing dinosaurs. Then it was lunchtime. Josie Smith didn't like her lunch. It smelled horrible and there were lumps in it and she'd forgotten to bring a paper bag in her pocket to hide them in. When she wouldn't eat the lumps the lunch lady shouted. Eileen was horrible as well because she wasn't friends with Josie Smith. School was horrible all day. In the afternoon they had to write a story, but Josie Smith couldn't remember any of the stories she'd made up in bed and as soon as she started writing, it went crooked and then she made a mistake. She couldn't borrow Eileen's pencil with an eraser on the end because they weren't friends, so she rubbed it out with her finger and made a hole in the page. Josie Smith wanted to go home. When it was time she ran all the way home by herself and in at her own front door.

"Where's your coat?" asked Josie's

mom, stopping her sewing machine. "You're wet through! Where's your coat?"

"Atchoo!" said Josie Smith. "Atchoo!"

"Oh, for goodness' sake," said Josie's mom. "You'll have tonsillitis again, next news. Come on, straight to bed."

Josie Smith went straight to bed and her mom brought her something to eat on a tray and said, "You'd better stay in bed tomorrow, just in case."

"Atchoo!" said Josie Smith. "Atchoo!"

Ginger stood up in his basket and stared at her.

"Will Ginger catch my cold?" asked Josie Smith.

"No," said Josie's mom.

"I'm glad I'm not going to school tomorrow," said Josie Smith. "I don't like it anymore."

"Why not?" asked Josie's mom. "You haven't been getting in trouble, have you?"

"No," said Josie Smith with her eyes shut.

"Well, why don't you want to go, then? Something must have happened."

"Eileen wouldn't lend me her pencil with an eraser on the end," said Josie Smith, "and I had to rub out with my finger and it made a hole."

"Is that all?" said Josie's mom.

"And I didn't like my lunch," said . Josie Smith.

And then they said good night.

The next morning it was raining again and Josie Smith stayed in bed. She heard the milkman come and she heard Eileen come and call for her and then go away again. She heard all the children going past to school and running and shouting in the yard far

away. Then she fell asleep again. After lunch, Josie's mom said she could get dressed and come down and color by the fire. Josie Smith came down. She sat by the fire with her crayons and coloring book and sometimes she listened to the rain pattering on the window and sometimes she listened to her mom's sewing machine going Tr-r-r-r-r-r-r-ik, tr-r-r-r-r-r-r-ik, tr-r-r-r-r-r-r-ik.

Then her mom said, "I'd better run across to Mrs. Chadwick's and get something for supper."

"Can I come?" said Josie Smith.

"No," said Josie's mom. "It's raining. You can watch me from the window."

So Josie Smith climbed on the chair by the window and watched her mom run across the street in the rain and go in Mrs. Chadwick's shop. Then she saw Mrs. Scowcroft. Mrs. Scowcroft went in Mrs. Chadwick's shop, too, and she had Josie Smith's coat over her arm. Josie Smith jumped down from the chair so that Mrs. Scowcroft wouldn't see her. She remembered that she'd been in Mr. Scowcroft's allotment garden when he wasn't there, and in his hen shed, and left her coat and been late for school. If Mrs. Scowcroft told on her she would get shouted at; she might get smacked. Josie Smith sat down on the rug. She didn't want to look out the window anymore. Then the door went Bam! And her mom came in. Josie Smith put her head down and looked at her coloring book.

"Well!" said Josie's mom. "I've been hearing some stories about you! Look what I've got here."

But Josie Smith didn't look because she knew it was her coat.

"I left it at Mr. Scowcroft's," she said.

"Look!" said Josie's mom.

Josie Smith looked. It wasn't her coat. It was a bunch of pom-pom dahlias. "Mrs. Scowcroft brought them for you, as well as your coat, to say thank you. Mr. Scowcroft's got bronchitis and she had to go and feed the hens for him yesterday. But when she got there somebody had fed them."

"Yes," said Josie Smith, and then she said, "I dug as well."

"And weren't you late for school?" asked Josie's mom.

"Yes," said Josie Smith.

"And is that why you were upset?" asked Josie's mom.

"I don't know," said Josie Smith. Then she said, "Can I take the pom-pom dahlias to school?"

"If you like," said Josie's mom. "Why don't you write a little story to take, as well?"

"All right," said Josie Smith.

So Josie Smith wrote a story by the fire and then she went to bed early. The next day, when Eileen came to call for her she

was ready with a ribbon in her hair and her
story and the bunch of pom-pom dahlias
and a note to say she'd been ill.

"What beautiful flowers," Miss Valentine said. "Are you better now?"

"Yes," said Josie Smith.

"And will you get all your arithmetic
problems right today?"

"Yes," said Josie Smith, shutting her
eyes tight because it was a lie.

"It's a shame you were away yesterday,"
Miss Valentine said, "because everybody

33

wrote a story and there's going to be a prize for the best one."

"I wrote a story," said Josie Smith, "with a giant and some Gypsies and a witch in it." And she gave her story to Miss Valentine.

Josie Smith liked school today. Miss Valentine helped her with her problems and Eileen lent her her pencil to erase with and they had potato chips for lunch.

When it was nearly home time, Miss Valentine said, "Everybody come and sit around me." Everybody went. Then she said: "Josie Smith, stand up."

Josie Smith stood up.

"Josie Smith wins the prize for the best story," Miss Valentine said.

"Josie Smith's always the best in the class at stories," Eileen said.

"And she's going to learn to be just as good at arithmetic," Miss Valentine said. "Isn't that right, Josie?"

"Yes," said Josie Smith, shutting her eyes because it was a lie.

"Here you are," Miss Valentine said.

Josie Smith opened her eyes. Then she opened them wider. Then she smiled a big smile and got tight hold of her prize. A shiny, stripy, brand new, sharpened pencil, with an eraser on the end.

Josie Smith and the Princess

Josie Smith and Eileen and Gary Grimes and Rawley Baxter were sitting at their table, reading.

"The princess was very sad as she walked among the flowers in the giant's garden," read Josie Smith.

"Today we are going to the seashore. We are going in the car," read Eileen.

"Here is a ball," read Rawley Baxter. "Play with the ball." And then he said, "Here is Batman! E-e-e-e-ow!" And he flew the plastic Batman from his pocket over all their books.

"House!" read Gary Grimes, and

turned a page. He was watching Rawley Baxter's Batman.

Everybody read louder and louder.

"Quietly," said Miss Valentine.

"'Princess, Princess, do not cry,' said the giant," read Josie Smith, "'for I will never hurt you.'"

"Can you see the sea?" read Eileen. "Can you see the waves?"

"E-e-e-c-e-ow!" said Rawley Baxter, not reading anything.

"Dog!" shouted Gary Grimes, and turned a page.

"Don't shout so loud," said Josie Smith.

"Quietly!" said Miss Valentine again.

Josie Smith finished her book but she didn't give it in. She didn't tell Miss Valentine that she'd finished it because she liked the book very much and she wanted to copy the picture of the princess with her white dress and long golden hair.

But Miss Valentine said: "Josie Smith, come and read to me."

Josie Smith went. She opened her book

in the middle and started reading. She hoped that Miss Valentine wouldn't notice that she'd read this bit before.

But Miss Valentine stopped her and said, "You read that part to me the other day. Haven't you finished this book yet?"

"No," said Josie Smith, shutting her eyes tight because it was a lie.

"Excuse me, Miss Valentine," said a big voice.

Josie Smith opened her eyes. It was Miss Potts, the principal, marching in. Josie Smith didn't like Miss Potts because she was always shouting, and when she shouted her face went all red and her eyes were glittery and frightening. But she didn't shout today.

"I've brought you a new little girl," she said, and she gave a piece of paper to Miss Valentine. Then she looked around and said: "Where is she?"

Josie Smith looked as well. And there was the most beautiful girl in the most beautiful dress that Josie Smith had ever seen.

"Come here to me," said the principal.

The girl came.

Josie Smith stared and stared. The girl
had smooth brown skin and big black eyes
and a braid that went right down to her
waist. Josie Smith had never seen a braid so
long. But the best of all was her dress. It was
soft and fine and it was an orangey pinky red
color like fire. All around the bottom of it
there were glittering stripes of gold, and
underneath it the girl wore fire-colored silky
trousers with gold stripes around her ankles.
In the new girl's ears there were tiny gold
earrings and she wore a gold bangle and a
ring.

Josie Smith thought she must be a princess. She stared and stared, holding her breath.

The principal went away and Miss Valentine said, "Now then, Tahara, we'd better find somebody to look after you."

"Can I look after her?" said Josie Smith. "Can I?"

Miss Valentine said, "I wanted you to help Gary Grimes with his reading."

"Can Eileen help Gary Grimes today? Can she?" asked Josie Smith. "And I'll look after...I'll look after..."

"Tahara," Miss Valentine said. "She's called Tahara Patel."

But Eileen came up to the desk and said, "Can I look after the new girl, Miss Valentine?"

"Can I look after her? Can I?" said all the other girls coming up to the desk.

"Well," said Miss Valentine. "Josie Smith asked first so she can look after Tahara today. Eileen, you can help Gary Grimes with his reading. Go and sit down, now, all of you. Quiet, everybody! Josie, get a chair from the library corner and put it at your table for Tahara." Josie Smith carried the chair over and put it next to her own and they sat down.

"Do you want me to read to you?" she said.

Tahara stared at Josie Smith with her big black eyes but she didn't say anything. Josie Smith opened her book at the first page. "Once upon a time there was a princess," she read, and she showed Tahara the picture. Tahara didn't say anything.

"House!" shouted Gary Grimes.

"That doesn't say house," Eileen said. "It says mother."

"Mother!" shouted Gary Grimes.

Tahara stared at Gary Grimes and then at Josie Smith and then at Josie Smith's book. Then she stared all around the room at the noisy children.

"Look," said Josie Smith, turning a page. "That's the giant's castle." But then Eileen nipped her hard on the arm.

"It's not fair," Eileen said, "because you're supposed to help Gary Grimes with his reading."

"Oh no I'm not," said Josie Smith.

"I'm supposed to look after Tahara. Miss Valentine said."

"She's horrible," Eileen said. "She's got horrible black hair."

"She has not!" said Josie Smith. "And it's longer than yours, anyway!"

"I don't care," Eileen said, "and I'm not playing with you at recess."

When recess came, Eileen got her coat and ran off but Josie Smith didn't care. She helped Tahara to find her jacket and they went out into the yard together.

"I'll hold your hand," said Josie Smith, and they walked around and around the edge of the yard near the railings. Josie Smith stared all the time at the glittery gold stripes around Tahara's dress and trousers. She would have liked to touch the gold and see what it felt like. When the big boys came close, shouting and kicking their football, Tahara stopped and held on to Josie Smith's hand very tight.

"Don't be frightened," said Josie Smith, "because if anybody pushes you or thumps you, I'll knock them down." And they went on walking around and around. Josie Smith told Tahara she was the best in the class at reading and writing stories. She told her that Eileen was horrible sometimes

and that she was her best friend. She told her that they could sit next to each other at lunchtime and she told her that she could come and watch television after school if she wanted to. Tahara didn't say anything.

Then they saw Eileen playing tag with the others. They stood and watched. Josie Smith liked playing tag. She wanted to run around and play.

"Shall we play, as well?" she said to Tahara. Tahara didn't say anything.

"Come on," said Josie Smith, and she pulled Tahara's hand. Tahara didn't come. She stood still and looked frightened.

"Do you not know how to play?" asked Josie Smith. "It's all right if you don't want to." Tahara held Josie Smith's hand tighter and they went on walking around and around until the whistle went and it was time to go in.

After recess they did some drawing. Josie Smith copied the princess from her reading book and showed it to Tahara.

"Aren't you drawing anything?" she said. –

Tahara looked at her piece of paper but

she didn't draw anything. Josie Smith said, "Do you want me to draw something for you?" She took Tahara's piece of paper and drew another princess. This one had a long black braid and a dress with trousers underneath. Josie Smith used her orange crayon and her pink crayon and her red crayon to color the dress.

"I haven't got a gold crayon," she told Tahara, "so I'll have to use my yellow for the stripes." She pointed at the stripes on Tahara's dress and then colored them on the picture with her yellow crayon. She gave the picture to Tahara. Tahara looked at it for a long time and then she looked at Josie Smith. Then she picked up her pencil very slowly and wrote something on the paper.

"Why are you writing back to front?" asked Josie Smith. But when she looked at what Tahara had written it didn't say anything. It was just squiggles and dots. "I can't read it if you write back to front," said Josie Smith.

But Tahara put her pencil down and pointed at the drawing. Then she looked at Josie Smith with her shiny black eyes.

"Tahara," she said, and she smiled.

At lunchtime, Josie Smith and Tahara sat next to each other. They had meat and potatoes and carrots.

"You have to try and eat it all," said Josie Smith, "or else the lunch lady shouts."

Tahara watched Josie Smith eating her lunch. Then she picked up her knife and fork very carefully and ate some carrots and potatoes. She didn't touch her meat.

"Do you not like meat?" asked Josie Smith. "I don't like it either but you have to eat some."

Tahara sat very still. The lunch lady came and saw Tahara's meat. She pointed at it and shouted, "Come on, now! You can at least eat some of it!"

"She doesn't like it," said Josie Smith.

"She can still eat a bit of it," the lunch lady said, and then she shouted at Gary Grimes for kicking carrots about under the table.

"Can't you eat just a little bit?" whispered Josie Smith to Tahara. But Tahara sat very still, staring at the noisy

children, and two big tears rolled down her cheeks.

"Don't cry," said Josie Smith. "I'll hide your meat for you." Josie Smith had a paper bag in her pocket from the kitchen drawer at home. She used it to hide the lumpy bits from her lunch that she didn't like. She took Tahara's meat and slid it into the bag in her pocket very carefully so that nobody saw.

Tahara stopped crying.

Then Miss Potts, the principal, marched in, shouting.

"Where's that new child?" she shouted, and she marched up to Josie Smith's table. "Where's the lunch lady for this table?" The lunch lady came. "This child," shouted the principal, "is not to eat meat. Her father told me this morning when he brought her and I meant to tell you before they started lunch but I was busy."

"Well, it's too late, now," said the lunch lady, and she looked at Tahara's plate. Then the principal and all the children at the table looked at Tahara's plate.

Josie Smith didn't look at Tahara's plate. She knew where the meat was but she didn't know if Tahara would tell.

"She's eaten it," the lunch lady said.

"Eaten it!" shouted the principal.

"I told her to eat it," said the lunch lady.

"Have you eaten your meat?" shouted the principal at Tahara, and she pointed at Tahara's plate, then at the meat on Gary Grimes's plate and then at Tahara's mouth. "Do you understand me?"

Tahara looked at Josie Smith.

"She's eaten it," said Josie Smith, shutting her eyes because it was a lie.

"Well, it can't be helped," the principal said, "but let's hope her father doesn't find out." Then she shouted at Rawley Baxter for playing with his plastic Batman at the table and went away.

When they were walking around the yard after lunch Josie Smith said to Tahara, "I'm glad you didn't tell."

Then Eileen came up to them with a girl called Ann Lomax and they stared at Tahara and giggled. Ann Lomax whispered something in Eileen's ear and then Eileen pointed at Tahara and said, "She's dumb because she wears trousers and a dress together."

"She is not!" shouted Josie Smith, and she tried to push Eileen over but Eileen and Ann Lomax ran away, giggling. Josie Smith ran after them but they went and stood near the teacher on duty so she couldn't hit them.

"Don't take any notice," Josie Smith told Tahara when she came back. Next time they passed Eileen, Josie Smith put her fist up and said, "If you don't leave her alone, I'll bash you after school!"

"A-aw! I'm going to tell on you for saying that," said Eileen.

"Tell-tale-tit!" roared Josie Smith.

In the afternoon, when it was story time, Miss Valentine said, "Everybody come and sit around me." And when they were sitting around, Miss Valentine leaned over and stroked Tahara's hair and smiled and said, "I wish I had your long hair."

Tahara didn't say anything but Josie Smith felt happy.

Then Miss Valentine gave everybody a

big piece of paper to take home. She told them to fold it down the middle and write a story on one half with a picture next to it. She told them that if they did their best they would get a gold star to stick on it and take home. Then she told them a little story and then it was time to go home.

"Good-af-ter-noon-Miss-Val-en-tine," the children said.

When they were putting their coats on, Tahara started to cry. She didn't roar like Josie Smith did when she cried. She didn't make any noise at all but big tears rolled down her cheeks and one of them splashed onto her sheet of white paper.

"What are you crying for?" asked Josie Smith.

Tahara didn't say anything.

Eileen and Ann Lomax said: "Crybaby, crybaby, in her dumb dress and trousers!"

When they went out, Tahara's dad was waiting at the gate. He saw the big tears rolling down Tahara's cheeks and he said something that Josie Smith couldn't understand. Tahara showed him the piece of paper and said a lot more things that Josie

Smith couldn't understand. Then Tahara's dad looked at Josie Smith and said, "What is it for, this paper?"

"She has to write a story on it," said Josie Smith, "and draw a picture."

They set off down the street together and at the corner before Josie Smith's house, Tahara and her dad stopped at a door.

"Is this your house?" asked Josie Smith. And then she said, "Can Tahara come to our house and watch television?"

But Tahara's dad shook his head and opened the door. Then he looked at Josie Smith and said, "You come here. Help Tahara, please." And he pointed at the paper.

"I'll ask my mom if I can come after supper," said Josie Smith, and she ran to the next corner as fast as she could and in at her own front door.

"Mom!" she shouted. "Mom! Can I go to Tahara's to help her with her story because tomorrow we're getting a gold star and can I have a braid in my hair for school?"

"Wash your hands," said Josie's mom.

"But *can* I?"

"Can you what? And wash your hands."

So Josie Smith washed her hands and told her mom all about Tahara. Then she said, "I'm going to be a princess when I grow up."

"I thought you were going to be a ballet dancer," said Josie's mom.

"I'm not anymore," said Josie Smith. "I'm being a princess because nobody can make you eat meat, not even Miss Potts. Mom? Why does Tahara's dad come to school and not her mom?"

"He works nights," said Josie's mom. "Mrs. Chadwick was telling me this morning in the shop. He does the shopping, too, she says, and Tahara's mom never goes out so nobody's seen her."

After supper Josie Smith put her coat on and got her pencil with an eraser on the end and her crayons.

"Can I go now?" she said.

"Don't be more than half an hour," said Josie's mom, "and put your scarf on."

Josie Smith put her scarf on and ran around the corner to Tahara's house.

Tahara's dad opened the door. When they
went into the kitchen, Tahara was sitting at
the table, ready with her sheet of paper, and
her mom was standing next to her, holding
a baby that was crying. Tahara's mom
wasn't smiling. She had creases in her
forehead like Josie's mom when she had a
headache. She had a long braid like
Tahara's.

"Sit down, please," said Tahara's dad.

"I've brought my pencil with an eraser
on the end and my crayons," said Josie
Smith.

Nobody said anything. Josie Smith took her coat and scarf off and sat down. Tahara looked at her with big shiny eyes. Then she touched the crayons.

"Go on," said Josie Smith. "Draw."

Tahara drew.

She drew something very big but Josie Smith couldn't tell what it was. Tahara's mom stood at one side of the table, rocking the baby that cried and watching with creases in her forehead. Her dad stood at the other side of the table and watched, leaning over to see.

Tahara drew.

"It's very tall," said Josie Smith, "and it's got a big nose like a giraffe but if it's going to be a giraffe it should have a straight neck and you've made it all bendy."

Tahara drew. She drew humps.

"I know what it is!" said Josie Smith. "It's a camel!"

Josie Smith started to write. *Once upon a time*, she wrote, *there was a...* then she stopped.

Tahara's mom and dad leaned over to look.

"Write," said Tahara's dad.

"I have to write camel," said Josie Smith.

"Can you write it?" asked Tahara's dad.

"I think I can," said Josie Smith, but she kept her eyes nearly shut when she said it because she didn't know whether she could write camel or not. She wrote *cam* and then she stopped. Tahara's dad stared at the paper and Tahara's mom stared at the paper. Even the baby stopped crying and stared at the paper.

"Is it finished?" asked Tahara's dad.

"Some of it is," said Josie Smith, "but there are some more letters that I can't remember. Will you help me?"

But Tahara's dad only shook his head and made creases in his forehead. "You try, please," he said.

Josie Smith tried. She tried so hard that she made creases in her forehead, too. She thought hard for a long time and then she finished the word. She wrote *cammle*. Then she looked at it and then she looked at Tahara's mom and dad.

They were both staring at the word but they didn't say anything.

Tahara drew. She drew some big
packages for the camel to carry on its back
and then she drew a man with a stick hitting
the camel.

"Hard work!" said Tahara's dad,
pushing Josie Smith's hand to make her
write.

The cammle worked very hard, wrote
Josie Smith.

Tahara drew big teardrops falling from
the camel's eyes.

"It's a sad story," said Josie Smith.
"Aren't you going to put a princess in it?"
But Tahara only stared at her with big
shiny eyes.

The cammle was very sad, wrote Josie
Smith.

"You could have a princess in it with a
dress like yours," she said.

Tahara's dad said something that Josie
Smith couldn't understand and Tahara
looked at Josie Smith and nodded.

Tahara drew. She drew a princess with
a long braid.

"And a dress like yours," said Josie

Smith, and she touched the golden stripes on Tahara's dress just a bit.

Tahara drew. Josie Smith wrote. *One day*, she wrote, *a princess saw the sad cammle.*

Then the story got happier. The camel ran away from the bad man with the stick and Tahara borrowed Josie Smith's pencil with an eraser on the end and rubbed out his tears and his packages. Then she drew a prince so that the princess wouldn't be by herself and they rode away on the camel's back together. At the end of the story, it was

nighttime and Tahara drew a moon and stars and colored the sky black all around them. Then she finished coloring the rest of the picture and Josie Smith wrote *And they all lived Happily ever afer. THE END.*

Then Tahara and her mom and dad all started talking at once and Tahara pointed to the princess's dress and the moon and stars and everybody looked at Josie Smith with creases in their foreheads.

"I haven't got a gold crayon," said Josie Smith, "or a silver one, either."

Tahara's mom said something and gave the baby to Tahara to hold. Then she went and got a bag from a drawer. It was like the bag that Josie's gran kept her knitting in, but it had better things in it than her gran's knitting bag, better even than her gran's button box, better even than her gran's magic handbag that always had a little present hidden in it for Josie Smith.

Tahara's mom emptied the bag onto the table and out spilled scraps of gold and silver cloth and pink and red see-through cloth and tiny see-through boxes with glittering sequins in them. Tahara's mom got some scissors and started cutting the scraps, and she made Tahara's dad bring a bit of glue in a rolled-up tube from a drawer.

Tahara sat quietly holding the baby and her mom started sticking the gold and silver scraps on the picture. She didn't have creases in her forehead anymore, she was laughing and talking fast. She stuck a gold dress on the princess and a silver moon in the sky. Then she stuck sequins on for stars.

Then there was a knock at the door. Bam, bam, bam.

Tahara's dad went to answer it. It was Josie's mom. Josie Smith had promised to go home in half an hour but then she forgot. She said good-bye and ran to the door with her coat and scarf. Josie's mom was nice and smiley to Tahara's dad, but when he went in and shut the door she said, "What did I tell you about coming home?"

"Not to be more than half an hour," said Josie Smith.

"And now it's more than half an hour past your bedtime," said Josie's mom. "You'll not play out again after supper!"

She marched Josie Smith home and

when they got there she said, "Straight to bed and no reading."

Josie Smith went straight to bed.

Ginger got in his basket next to Josie Smith's bed and Josie's mom turned the light off.

In the dark, Josie Smith whispered to Ginger, "Do you want me to tell you a story? It's a good story with a camel and a princess in it." She started off, "Once upon a time..." and then she stopped and sat up. "I haven't written my own story," she said. "I've forgotten it!"

Her own sheet of paper was downstairs in the kitchen where she'd left it before supper and there was nothing written on it at all! Josie Smith got out of bed with her chest going bam, bam, bam, and crept downstairs in her striped pajamas.

"What are you doing out of bed?" said Josie's mom. She was still mad.

"I've got to write a story and draw a picture for school. Miss Valentine said."

"Never you mind what Miss Valentine said. Go back to bed this minute and get to sleep."

"I've got to give it in tomorrow," said Josie Smith, "and we're getting a gold star."

"Well you'll have to give it in another day. It's your own fault for staying out late. Now get up those stairs!"

Josie Smith went back to bed. In the dark she started crying. Ginger heard her crying and jumped on the bed to put his nose near hers. Josie Smith sat up and got hold of him tight.

"What am I going to do, Ginger?" said Josie Smith. "If I go down again my mom will shout, and if I go to school without my story Miss Valentine will shout."

Josie Smith cried and cried and Ginger

purred and licked her wet cheeks and then they both fell asleep.

The next day at school, everybody gave in their sheets of paper and made a big pile on Miss Valentine's desk, all except Gary Grimes who'd lost his. Josie Smith's paper was at the bottom of the pile so you couldn't see there was nothing written on it. Josie Smith forgot about it and played with Tahara. They didn't play with Eileen because she said Tahara was horrible.

When they came back after lunch, Miss Valentine said, "Everybody come and sit around me."

Everybody came. Miss Valentine got the pile of papers and her little box of gold stars and Josie Smith's chest started going bam, bam, bam. Miss Valentine gave them back their papers. They all got one and they all got a gold star, even Rawley Baxter who'd done a drawing of Batman with hardly any writing. All except Gary Grimes and Josie Smith. Miss Valentine didn't say anything to Gary Grimes and Josie Smith. She only said, "I'm very pleased with all the stories but there's one very special one that I want to show to all of you."

She took Tahara's paper from her and held it up.

"Ooooooh!" said all the children, as they stared at Tahara's picture with the golden clothes and the silver moon and sequins glittering in the black sky. "Ooooooh!"

"Isn't it beautiful?" said Miss Valentine, "and it's a very good story, too. Well done, Tahara. I think everybody should clap for her."

Everybody clapped. Tahara sat very still with her paper on her knee.

"You can take your stories home with

you at home time. Now go back to your places and get your reading books out. And Eileen and Josie, change places so that Eileen can help Tahara, while I hear Josie read.''

Eileen sat in Josie Smith's chair and put her arm around Tahara and said, "It's nice, your picture. If you'll be my friend I'll give you a whole bag of caramels.''

Josie Smith went to read. When she'd read, Miss Valentine said, "Why didn't you write me a story like the others, Josie?''

A big lump came into Josie Smith's throat and tears came into her eyes.

"Because my mom..." The big lump stopped the words coming out. She tried to say, "Because my mom said I had to go to bed," but the words were all squashed and jumpy with crying.

"Don't cry," Miss Valentine said, and she wiped Josie Smith's tears with a tissue from the box on her desk.

"Blow," she said.

Josie Smith blew.

"Now then," said Miss Valentine, "can you spell camel?''

"Yes," said Josie Smith with her eyes shut.

"Go on then," said Miss Valentine.

"C-a-m," said Josie Smith, then she thought for a bit and said, "m-l-e."

"I thought as much," Miss Valentine said. "I was sure that was your writing on Tahara's paper. You wrote her story for her, didn't you?"

"It was Tahara's story," said Josie Smith. "I only wrote it down for her because she writes back to front and it comes out all squiggly so you can't read it."

"It's a different sort of writing," said Miss Valentine, "with different letters, that's why you can't read it. Do you understand?''

"Yes," said Josie Smith with her eyes shut tight.

"I'm very pleased with you for helping Tahara," Miss Valentine said, "and I know you like stars. I can't give you a gold star because it wouldn't be fair when you didn't bring a story but here's a silver star for you for being a kind helper."

Josie Smith took the silver star and went and sat down.

When it was recess, all the girls crowded around Tahara. They touched her dress and her long braid and wanted to be her friend. Eileen asked her to swap some sequins for candy. Tahara stared at them with her big black eyes and didn't say anything. Josie Smith stood near them by the railings. She felt the silver star in her pocket near the bag of lumps from her lunch. She wanted to throw the horrible silver star in the trash can and cry. She didn't want to be a kind helper, she wanted to be the best in the class at stories.

Everybody crowded around Tahara

and her dad going home, as well. Josie Smith walked behind them by herself. When they got to Tahara's house, the others went on but Tahara and her dad stopped and waited for Josie Smith. When she caught up Tahara got hold of her hand.

"Come in, please," said Tahara's dad.

"I can't," said Josie Smith. "My mom said I've got to go straight home or I'll get shouted at."

"Yes. Good," said Tahara's dad. "Wait here, please."

He went in and Tahara stood holding Josie Smith's hand. Then Tahara's mom came. She didn't come outside, she stood behind the door and made a sign with her finger. Tahara took Josie Smith inside and Tahara's mom held something up, talking fast. It was a long see-through scarf, very big, and it was the color of fire, like Tahara's dress, with glittering gold stripes all along it. She wrapped it around and around Josie Smith's head and shoulders and said a lot of things that Josie Smith couldn't understand, and smiled.

Josie Smith's chest went bam, bam,

bam, and she was so excited that she nearly forgot to say thank you. She ran down the street as fast as her rubber boots would go and in at her own front door.

"Mom!" she shouted. "Mom! Look at me!" And she whizzed around and around as fast as she could to make the fiery golden scarf fly up. "Do I look nice? Do I?"

"You look beautiful!" said Josie's mom, catching her and lifting her up high. "Just like a little princess!"

Josie Smith and the Concert

"We're having a concert!" shouted Josie Smith, running in from school and banging the door.

"Don't bang the door," said Josie's mom. "How many times have I told you?"

"I forgot," said Josie Smith. "Mom, we're having a concert at school and our class is doing a play and we're all in it!"

"Don't shout," said Josie's mom. "I can hear you."

"We're going to be fairies," said Josie Smith, "and the boys are being elves and there's a fairy queen and a fairy king and another thing that I've forgotten and

Tahara's going to be it. Mom?"

"What?"

"When will my hair be as long as Tahara's?"

"It takes years and years for hair to grow as long as Tahara's."

"As long as Eileen's, then?"

"I don't know. What's happened to your ribbon?"

Josie Smith felt her tiny braid. "I've lost it," she said.

"Again!" said Josie's mom. "Go and wash your hands. You're filthy."

"I want to tell you about the concert," said Josie Smith.

"You can tell me while you wash your hands," said Josie's mom.

"We're having dresses made of crepe paper," said Josie Smith, "and paper flowers in our hair and the boys are having paper hats with pointed ears stuck on. Will you make my costume?"

"I'll probably end up making more than just yours," said Josie's mom, "if it's anything like last year's nativity play."

"That's because you're good at sewing," said Josie Smith. "Mom? I'm hungry and thirsty."

"Well, help me to set the table, then."

Josie Smith helped.

After supper she went next door to Eileen's and played.

Eileen said: "My mom's buying all the crepe paper for all the costumes and some flowers for the stage. Only, you're not to tell anybody because it's a secret."

The next day, at school, they practiced one of their songs for the concert. They practiced in the cafeteria after lunch while the lunch ladies were stacking the tables and everything smelled of cabbage and the windows were steamed up because it was raining.

All the girls wanted Miss Valentine to say who was going to be the fairy queen but Miss Valentine said, "I haven't decided yet."

At recess, the girl called Ann Lomax came up and whispered to Josie Smith. "Do you want to know a secret?" she said.

"Yes," said Josie Smith.

Ann Lomax wasn't Josie Smith's

friend. She sat at another table. She had a kilt like Josie Smith's, only yellow, and she had blond hair and sometimes she had specks of red on her nails because her mom let her play with nail polish at home.

Ann Lomax put her hands around her mouth and whispered hard in Josie Smith's ear and made it feel hot.

"You won't tell?" she whispered.

"No," said Josie Smith.

"Eileen's mom came to school at lunchtime."

"Well?" said Josie Smith.

"Sh! You're not to tell anybody! She brought some stuff for the concert and one of the lunch ladies heard her say, 'If our Eileen's not the fairy queen there'll be trouble.'"

And Ann Lomax ran away.

Josie Smith played with Eileen. When the whistle went and they were lining up, Eileen whispered to Josie Smith, "It's between you and me who's going to be the queen, my mom said."

The next day at lunch time it was raining again when they practiced their song in the hall. The big windows were steamed up and everything smelled of stew. When they'd finished singing, Miss Valentine made them all go up on the stage and stand in a line.

"Boys on this side and girls on that side," she said.

Then she looked at them all and said: "Who's the tallest of you boys?"

The boys all said: "Rawley Baxter!"

"And who's the tallest girl?"

The girls all said: "Julie Horrocks!"

"Rawley Baxter and Julie Horrocks, come and stand in the middle," said Miss Valentine.

Rawley Baxter and Julie Horrocks stood in the middle and Miss Valentine said, "Because you're the tallest, you're going to be the fairy king and queen."

Rawley Baxter said, "I don't want to."

Julie Horrocks didn't say anything. She had long thin legs and big glasses and bangs and she was almost as tall as Rawley Baxter.

"She doesn't look like a fairy queen," whispered Eileen. "And anyway, she's ugly because she's got glasses."

"All the fairies stand in a circle around

the fairy queen," said Miss Valentine, "and now, sit down on the floor."

When they were sitting down, Eileen whispered to Josie Smith, "And anyway, when we did the nativity play in the baby class, Julie Horrocks wet her pants and the angel next to her slipped in the puddle."

Josie Smith didn't say anything. She pointed at the fairy king when Miss Valentine said to point, and she sang. She liked being a fairy.

At home time, Eileen said, "I'm going to tell my mom I don't want to be in the concert."

Josie Smith ran in at her own front door.

"Mom!" she shouted, "Julie Horrocks is being the fairy queen because she's the tallest, and she's got bangs and glasses."

"Wash your hands," said Josie's mom, "and your face, while I finish sewing this seam. I don't know how you manage to get so filthy at school."

"We had to sit on the floor," said Josie Smith, "when we were practicing our play for the concert."

"What's it about?" asked Josie's mom.

"I don't know," said Josie Smith. "We have to point at the fairy king and sing a song. Mom, Julie Horrocks is the queen and she hasn't even got blond curly hair like Eileen."

Josie's mom put her sewing away and started cooking something.

"Are you upset because you're not the queen?" she asked.

"No," said Josie Smith. "I like being a fairy." But then she said, "I wish I had bangs like Julie Horrocks."

"I thought you wanted to grow your hair like Tahara's," said Josie's mom.

"I do," said Josie Smith, "but I want bangs, as well."

"It could do with cutting," said Josie's mom, and she stroked Josie Smith's hair. "It's so untidy. If you really want to grow it we should trim it all to the same length and then it'll grow nicely."

"And cut me bangs?" asked Josie Smith.

"All right," said Josie's mom.

So, after supper, Josie Smith sat on a

chair in front of the fire with a towel tucked around her neck and newspapers around her feet, and her mom cut her hair.

Snick, snick, snick, went Josie's mom around the back of her neck.

"It tickles," said Josie Smith.

"Keep still."

Snick, snick, snick, went Josie's mom around her ears.

"Mom," said Josie Smith, "Julie Horrocks wet her pants on the stage when we were in the baby class."

"I know she did. I remember."

"And then she cried, didn't she? She cries when we have a spelling test, as well."

"She's very highly strung," said Josie's mom.

"Is that why her legs are so long?" asked Josie Smith, "and she never plays outside?"

"She's shy because she's so tall," said Josie's mom. "You should call for her sometimes."

"I did call for her," said Josie Smith, "and she wouldn't play outside and we went in her bedroom and she keeps all her toys in a line on the shelf and she doesn't play with them. When are you going to cut my bangs?"

"In a minute. Keep still."

"Do you want me to sing you the song that we're practicing at school?"

"If you want, only keep your head still."

"I am keeping it still," said Josie Smith, and then she sang:

"You spo-otte-ed snakes with dou-ou-bl-le tongues, thorn-y hedgehogs co-ome not near!"

Snick, went Josie's mom, snick, snick, snick.

"Come not near our fairy queen!" sang Josie Smith.

Snick, went Josie's mom, snick, snick, snick.

"Lulla-lulla-lulla-by," sang Josie Smith.

Snick, went Josie's mom, snick, snick, snick.

"I can't remember any more," said Josie Smith.

"Keep really still, now," said Josie's mom, "and shut your eyes." And the cold scissors went nipping across Josie Smith's forehead making little bangs. Snick, snick, snick.

When she'd finished, the newspapers on the floor around Josie Smith's chair had little snips of hair all over them. Josie's mom threw the snips of hair into the fire and they sizzled. Then she let Josie Smith stand on the chair to look in the mirror. Josie Smith smiled.

"I like my bangs," she said. "Can I have a curl in them?"

"No," said Josie's mom. "You'll never get to sleep with a roller in your hair. It'll hurt you."

"But for the concert, can I?"

"All right," said Josie's mom. "Just for the concert. Now, get ready for bed."

Josie Smith got ready for bed, and in the bathroom she stood on the stool to look in the mirror again and see if her bangs were still there, and she smiled. When she was in bed and her mom had switched the light off and gone down, she felt for her bangs in the dark. They were nice and smooth. "I've got

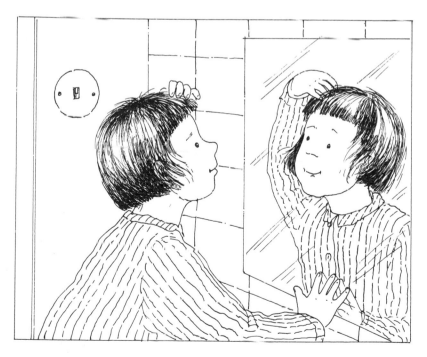

bangs," she whispered to Ginger in his basket by the bed.

"Eeeiow," said Ginger.

Josie Smith sang a bit of her song for Ginger very quietly in the dark. Ginger purred. When she couldn't remember any more, Josie Smith and Ginger fell asleep.

In the morning, when Eileen came to call for her to go to school, Josie Smith said: "I've got bangs."

"It's short, your hair," Eileen said. "It makes you look like a boy."

"It doesn't," said Josie Smith, "and anyway, when it's the concert I'm having curls."

At lunchtime, when they practiced in the hall, it was raining hard again and they had to have the lights on. The big windows were all steamed up and everything smelled of fish. After the song they went up on the stage and Miss Valentine said, "Today, you're going to learn a little dance. First of all, divide into pairs, a fairy and an elf to each pair."

They all started arguing and pushing and making a terrible noise and then Miss

Potts came marching into the hall and shouted. She stopped with her hands on her hips and her face all red and said, "You children are making far too much noise! I can hear the row you're making from my office!"

Miss Valentine said quietly, "Come on, now, make your pairs. It doesn't matter who you choose, you can always change later."

But the children all shouted: "Miss Valentine, there aren't enough elves!"

"Oh dear," said Miss Valentine. "There are two boys away."

And the children all shouted: "Miss Valentine, and they're having their tonsils out and they won't be back for the concert!"

And they all started arguing and pushing again.

"Will you be quiet!" roared Miss Potts, and she stamped on to the stage shouting, "I'll see to this, Miss Valentine!"

And she started pushing the children about, roaring: "Stand still! Go over there! You come to the front where we can see you! Be quiet!" Then she shouted: "Eileen, stand here! Now, Josie Smith, come to me! You've

got the shortest hair of all the girls so you can be an elf! Come and stand here next to Eileen!''

Josie Smith went. Her chest was going bam, bam, bam, but she didn't say anything. She was frightened of Miss Potts.

Miss Potts stamped down off the stage, shouting, ''A lot of fuss about nothing! And don't let me hear this class making a noise again! Practice quietly!'' And she marched away.

Josie Smith stood next to Eileen with her chest going bam, bam, bam, and her face all hot, waiting for Miss Valentine to send her back to her own side to be a fairy. But Miss Valentine didn't say anything. She wasn't smiling like she usually did and nobody liked practicing anymore. Everybody did the dance wrong and Josie Smith couldn't even sing anymore because she had a big lump in her throat.

In the afternoon, instead of a story, Miss Valentine told them about the play. She said that Tahara was a child stolen by the queen from the prince of a faraway land and changed into a fairy and that she wouldn't need a costume because she could wear one of her own beautiful dresses with golden stripes and trousers underneath, because Tahara came from a faraway land like the stolen child. She said that the fairies would dance in their bare feet and have paper flowers on their hands as well as in their hair and that the elves, as well as having paper hats and tunics, had to wear woolly tights borrowed from their sisters or moms.

When they were putting their coats on at home time, Miss Valentine came and put her hand on Josie Smith's head and stroked her bangs and said, "Thank you for being an elf, Josie. The dance will look much nicer with the same number of elves and fairies. You don't mind not being a fairy, do you?"

"No," said Josie Smith, shutting her eyes tight because it was a lie.

Out in the yard, Eileen and Ann Lomax pulled Josie Smith's bangs and said, "Josie Smith's a boy! Josie Smith's a boy!"

Josie Smith put her head down and ran as fast as her rubber boots would go down the street and in at her own front door.

"What's the matter with you?" said Josie's mom. "You're all red in the face."

"I don't like Miss Valentine anymore," said Josie Smith.

"Has she been shouting at you?" said Josie's mom.

"No," said Josie Smith.

"Run across to Mrs. Chadwick's for me," said Josie's mom, "and get a quarter pound of boiled ham for supper, there's a

good girl. And afterward you can help me with the fairies' costumes."

"I don't want to," said Josie Smith.

"I'm going to make some tiny flowers with loops to fit on their fingers," said Josie's mom. "You'll like doing that."

Josie Smith didn't say anything. She ran across to Mrs. Chadwick's for the boiled ham and after supper she helped her mom with the paper flowers. She didn't want to tell her mom that she wasn't being a fairy anymore. She didn't even tell Ginger at bedtime. She didn't want to tell anybody.

She lay in bed in the dark and pulled and pulled at her short hair until it hurt so much that she cried, and she hated her mom for cutting it.

On the last day before the concert there were people practicing in the hall all day. Josie Smith could hear the piano from her classroom when she was doing her arithmetic, and when she was reading she could hear another class saying a poem all together. Josie Smith's class had to practice after lunch. Josie Smith's mom and some other moms were bringing all the costumes to try on.

When it was time, they lined up and Miss Valentine took them into the hall. The wall at the back of the stage was all covered over with black crepe paper with stars and a moon stuck on. Josie Smith's chest went bam, bam, bam, because, even if she couldn't be a fairy, she was still excited because of the concert. Everybody else was excited, too, and when they started to get undressed they were all falling over each other and pushing and giggling and losing their clothes and Miss Valentine couldn't keep them quiet. Josie Smith didn't get ready. She didn't want to. She looked at the table where the fairies' dresses were and saw a heap of big paper flowers and a heap of small ones, yellow and white and purple. But then somebody's mom got hold of Josie Smith and started undressing her and somebody else's mom tried a paper hat on her with a pointy top and pointy paper ears stuck on the sides and pulled it right down over her bangs. Then the mom smiled and said, "You do look comic."

Josie Smith went into a corner at the

back near the stage. She sat down with her legs crossed and started crying. At first she tried not to make any noise so that nobody would notice, but then she cried louder and louder because she couldn't help it, and nobody noticed anyway because they were all shouting and talking and pushing and arguing and losing their shoes and ripping their paper costumes. Even Josie's mom didn't notice. But all of a sudden a loud voice said:

"Who's that crying?"

Josie Smith pulled the elf's hat further down over her bangs and put her head down on her knees with her eyes shut. Everybody stopped shouting and pushing and stood still to listen. Josie Smith listened, too, but she didn't hear anybody say, "Josie Smith's crying." Instead, she heard a boy's voice roaring.

"Wa-a-a-a-a-a-ah! Wa-a-a-a-a-a-ah! Wa-a-a-a-a-a-ah!"

And then somebody said, "It's Rawley Baxter!"

Josie Smith opened her eyes. Everybody was staring at Rawley Baxter. He was

standing in the middle of the hall in woolly tights and a green paper cloak and a gold paper crown with his eyes shut tight and his mouth wide open, roaring.

"Wa-a-a-a-a-a-ah! Wa-a-a-a-a-a-ah! Wa-a-a-a-a-a-ah!" roared Rawley Baxter. "Wa-a-a-a-a-a-ah! Wa-a-a-a-a-a-ah! Wa-a-a-a-a-ah!"

Miss Valentine said, "Whatever's the matter?"

She went and put her arm around him but Rawley Baxter pushed her away and then slapped and whacked at his green paper cloak, trying to get it off, and roaring, "Wa-a-a-a-a-a-ah! Wa-a-a-a-a-a-ah! Wa-a-a-a-a-a-ah!"

"Tell me, what's the matter?" said Miss Valentine.

But Rawley Baxter wouldn't tell.

Ann Lomax knew what was the matter and she told.

"Miss Valentine, he doesn't want to be a fairy king because it's sissy. Miss Valentine, he only likes being Batman and he doesn't want to be dressed up in a green cloak."

"Oh dear," said Miss Valentine, but before she could do anything about it, the children all shouted:

"Miss Valentine! Miss Valentine! Julie Horrocks is crying, as well!"

Everybody looked at Julie Horrocks. She was standing on the stage in her white paper dress and her big glasses and with her long thin legs, going, "Ooomp! Ooomp! Ooomp!" and big tears were rolling down her face.

"Whatever's the matter?" asked Miss Valentine.

"Ooomp!" said Julie Horrocks. "Ooomp! Ooomp! Ooomp!" and she wouldn't tell.

Ann Lomax knew what was the matter and she told.

"Miss Valentine, it's because she's got to stand at the front because she's the queen and everybody will see that she's too tall so she wants to stand at the back and be an ordinary fairy."

"Ooomp!" sobbed Julie Horrocks. "Ooomp! Ooomp! Ooomp!"

"Wa-a-a-a-a-a-ah!" roared Rawley Baxter. "Wa-a-a-a-a-a-ah! Wa-a-a-a-a-a-ah! Wa-a-a-a-a-ah!"

"Oh dear," said Miss Valentine, but before she could do anything about it, all the children shouted:

"Miss Valentine! Miss Valentine! Eileen's crying as well!"

Everybody looked at Eileen. She was leaning against the wall with her face in her hands, going: "Meh-heh-heh! Meh-heh-heh! Meh-heh-heh!" as loud as she could.

"What's the matter with you?" said Miss Valentine.

"Meh-heh-heh!" wailed Eileen. "Meh-heh-heh! Meh-heh-heh! Meh-heh-heh" and she wouldn't tell.

Ann Lomax knew and she told.

"Miss Valentine, it's because she wants to be the fairy queen, her mom promised her she would be, because she's got golden curls."

"Meh-heh-heh!" wailed Eileen against the wall. "Meh-heh-heh! Meh-heh-heh! Meh-heh-heh!"

"Ooomp!" sobbed Julie Horrocks on the stage. "Ooomp! Ooomp! Ooomp!"

"Wa-a-a-a-a-ah!" roared Rawley Baxter in the middle of the hall. "Wa-a-a-a-a-a-ah! Wa-a-a-a-a-a-ah! Wa-a-a-a-a-a-ah!"

"Oh dear," said Miss Valentine, but before she could do anything about it, all the children shouted:

"Miss Valentine! Miss Valentine! Tahara's crying as well."

Everybody looked at Tahara.

Tahara was in the middle of all the fairies, wearing her fire-colored dress and trousers with golden stripes. She hardly made any noise at all but tears were rolling

97

down her face from her big black eyes and
every so often she went: "Nff! Nff! Nff!"

"Tahara," said Miss Valentine. "Whatever's the matter with you?"

"Nff!" went Tahara quietly. "Nff! Nff!
Nff!" and she wouldn't tell.

Ann Lomax knew and she told.

"Miss Valentine, it's because she has to
wear her own dress and she wants a paper
costume like Josie Smith."

"Nff!" sniffed Tahara in the middle of
the fairies. "Nff! Nff! Nff!"

"Meh-heh-heh!" wailed Eileen against
the wall. "Meh-heh-heh! Meh-heh-heh!
Meh-heh-heh!"

"Ooomp!" sobbed Julie Horrocks on the stage. "Ooomp! Ooomp! Ooomp!"

"Wa-a-a-a-a-ah!" roared Rawley Baxter in the middle of the hall. "Wa-a-a-a-a-ah! Wa-a-a-a-a-h! Wa-a-a-a-a-ah!"

Josie Smith cried a bit harder to join in but nobody noticed her in her corner on the floor.

"Oh dear," said Miss Valentine.

Then Josie's mom went up to Rawley Baxter.

"Wa-a-a-a-a-ah!" Rawley Baxter roared.

"Listen," said Josie's mom.

"Wa-a-a-a-a-a-ah!" said Rawley Baxter.

"Listen," said Josie's mom, and she took the green cloak off him. "We've got some black crepe paper left over from the sky. If you want I'll make you a black cloak and afterward you can use it to be Batman."

Rawley Baxter stopped crying.

"Can I wear my Batman mask with the cloak in the concert as well?" he said.

Josie's mom looked at Miss Valentine.

"All right," said Miss Valentine, "as long as he wears the gold crown, too."

Rawley Baxter smiled.

Then Josie's mom went up on the stage.

"Ooomp!" said Julie Horrocks.

"Listen," said Josie's mom.

"Ooomp!" said Julie Horrocks.

"Listen," said Josie's mom. "You don't have to be the fairy queen if you're too frightened, does she, Miss Valentine?"

"I suppose not," said Miss Valentine.

Julie Horrocks stopped crying.

"You can be a fairy," said Josie's mom,

"and stand near the back where nobody can see your legs."

Julie Horrocks smiled.

"Give me your crown," said Josie's mom, and she came down off the stage and went over to Eileen.

"Meh-heh-heh!" said Eileen.

"Listen," said Josie's mom.

"Meh-heh-heh!" said Eileen.

"Listen," said Josie's mom. "Julie Horrocks doesn't want to be the queen anymore and I'm sure if you stop crying Miss Valentine will let you be the queen instead, won't you, Miss Valentine?"

"All right," said Miss Valentine.

Eileen stopped crying.

"Look," said Josie's mom. "Here's your silver crown. You can change into the white dress afterward." And she put the silver crown on Eileen's golden curls.

Eileen smiled.

"Now," said Josie's mom. "What are we going to do about Tahara?"

"Nff," said Tahara.

"What do you want to be?" asked Josie's mom.

"Nff!" said Tahara.

"She doesn't want to wear her own dress," Ann Lomax said.

"Does anybody else want to wear Tahara's dress?" asked Josie's mom.

"I do," Ann Lomax said.

"And what does Miss Valentine say?" asked Josie's mom.

"I wanted Tahara to be the stolen child," Miss Valentine said, "because she's supposed to be dark and come from a far-away land." But then she said, "Oh dear. All right."

"I can put makeup on," Ann Lomax said. "My mom lets me sometimes."

"All right," Miss Valentine said, and Josie's mom took Tahara's dress off her and gave it to Ann Lomax.

Ann Lomax smiled.

"What do you want to wear, Tahara?" asked Josie's mom.

Tahara pointed and everybody looked where she was pointing.

She was pointing at Josie Smith in her elf's hat, sitting cross-legged in the corner.

"Josie," said Josie's mom. "Come here a minute, will you?"

Josie came. She wasn't crying anymore now that nobody else was.

"I didn't know you were being an elf," said Josie's mom. "But now Tahara wants your costume. Will you let her wear it?"

"Yes," said Josie Smith.

"You can wear Ann Lomax's fairy costume," said Josie's mom.

"Yes," said Josie Smith, and she took off her elf's hat and gave it to Tahara.

Tahara smiled. Then she stroked the paper ears.

"Here you are," said Josie's mom, and she gave Josie Smith the flowers for her hair and fingers.

Josie Smith smiled.

"Has everybody stopped crying?" asked Miss Valentine.

"Yes!" shouted all the children.

"Well, thank goodness for that," said Miss Valentine.

And the next night when all the moms and dads were in their seats in the hall and Josie Smith was waiting to go on the stage with her fairy dress and flowers and a curl in her bangs, Miss Valentine came and put her arm around her and said, "I wanted to say thank you to you, Josie, for not being selfish. I don't think you really liked being an elf, did you?"

"No," said Josie Smith.

"But you didn't make a fuss and cry like Eileen and the others did."

"No," said Josie Smith with her eyes half shut.

"I don't know how I would have managed," Miss Valentine said, "without

you and your mom. All right, are you ready to go on?"

"Yes," said Josie Smith, pointing her toe and holding her paper skirt out with flowery fingers.

"Shh!" said Miss Valentine to all the elves and fairies. "It's time!"

When they went on the stage they all waved to their moms and dads and Josie Smith waved to her mom and her gran and then they remembered to sing

Josie Smith felt so shiny and happy that she sang twice as loud as she'd ever sung before.

"Come not near our fairy queen!" she sang, and Eileen lay down to sleep with her eyes shut tight and the silver crown on her golden curls.

"Lul-la-by," sang Josie Smith, "lul-la-by! Lul-lu-la-by!"